Devenir Nous

(translated *Becoming Us*)

a collection of wedding poems

by Nicole M. Southern

Devenir Nous

Books may be purchased in quantity and/or special sales by contacting the publisher, Nicole M. Southern, by email at nicolemsouthern.author@gmail.com.

First Edition

Published in the United States of America by Nicole M. Southern

Table of Contents

Foreword

The process of becoming one from two is described and indicated four separate times in the Bible. This is not by any means an accident. We know very well that God is intentional, and for this reason, we know even numbers have significance. The number four is biblically significant for creation. So, four different times it is noted that, *"Man shall leave his father and mother and be joined to his wife, and the two shall become one flesh."*

Genesis 2:24,
Matthew 19:5,
Mark 10:8,
and **Ephesians 5:31**

Transitioning from two to one is not an instantaneous process and should not be taken lightly. As individuals, there were needs and wants, strengths and weaknesses that would and should change in the midst of this marital transformation. Should we submit to the process, position ourselves for the shedding of things, the process becomes very beautiful. It resembles the changing of a caterpillar into a butterfly. How? The caterpillar is a different entity and it literally liquifies within the chrysalis and is reborn into a new creature that emerges, transformed and beautiful. The old self died and a new one was born. Likewise, marriage is intended to bring about a new creation that completes and reflects the image of God.

"And God said, let us make man in our image, after our likeness…" **Genesis 1:26**

When God began to speak to me about marriage, one of the things He specified for me was that I should be baptized with my husband when my "appointed time" comes. He clarified for me that baptism was an outward expression / declaration of the inner and spiritual transfiguration (this was also the case when I gave my life to Christ and was baptized as an individual). This second baptism, however, was in declaration of the death of "me" as an individual (as well as my husband), and to declare our rebirth as one flesh. "We are no longer two, but now are one."

I was recently reading about Jewish wedding traditions and two things in particular were highlighted for me. One was an article I received via email that indicated after the couple has wed, it's traditional for them to take a walk together holding hands. This, in my mind, is sweet and romantic. It also reminded me of all those times I watched my grandparents go for a walk together holding hands after dinner (three miles they would walk and after my grandmother died, my grandfather would continue to walk it at the mall for exercise. He would drive there and walk around the mall every day. The biblical significance of the number three is perfected and completed through a process). So, it made sense to me that my husband and I should do this together when our time comes.

The other, similar thing that was highlighted for me is called "yichud," which means "seclusion." Prior to marriage, the couple is not allowed to be in seclusion without a "Shomer" (we would generally call them a chaperone, but the Shomer is more strategically positioned with more of an understanding for the need of our obedience. God's laws are sacred and must be obeyed without compromise). After the marriage ceremony, the couple is led into the yichud chamber and they are left alone for a minimum of eight minutes (eight being biblically significant for new beginnings). Within the chamber is food, drink, etc. The door is locked from the inside and the couple is allowed to spend time together without being disturbed, so as to allow for them to transition from being "two individuals" to "one flesh" before they rejoin their guests to celebrate. It is imperative that they are able to transition from, "what I need," as an individual, to "what we need" as one flesh, so the marriage can flourish. Many marriages could have benefited from this process, along with marriage / premarital counseling prior to getting married.

For some, I have thought that having children ahead of time (although not God's perfect plan for us, but very common in our everyday life) would make it clear for them that, "it is no longer about them", and now about "the child." For those couples who are able to embrace this understanding, it might become clearer for them in such circumstances. However, more often than not, having a child is not enough to get us beyond our selfishness any more than getting married without understanding. We still collectively need an opportunity to learn and embrace the significance of changing from two single individuals to becoming one in marriage.

Many married people say, “Marriage is a full-time job,” but I will tell you that this was not God’s plan or intention for this institution. Everything God made was designed to reflect God and glorify Him. Because I’m aware of this truth, I have said for years that, “Marriage is worship / marriage is ministry.” God has spent forty-eight years teaching me, but more specifically the last twenty-two years making sure I understand this fact:

A wife loves God through her husband and a husband loves God through his wife. They do everything “for His glory and then also for our good.” What does that mean? I need to love you beyond you, just like Jesus loves me beyond me. The bible says that, “while we were enemies, Christ died for us.” Romans 5:8,10. What we do for one another should not

be based on a single moment. If you made me feel good today, or if you were getting on my nerves, it should be based on who God says we are and how much we trust God. That shouldn't change one day to the next, if we love God and trust Him, because He is the same now and forever. Our love for one another should reflect that love God first gives us. Likewise, God told me, that, "What I want my husband to give to me, I must first give it to him." This makes perfect sense when you understand and submit to its reflection. It goes all the way back to one of our most cherished songs as a child:
Oh, how I love Jesus, because He first loved me.

Devenir Nous is French that translates into English, "Becoming Us." This collection of poems is intended to describe that process and also to aid in the revelation of that transformation. It was God's request for me to have these poems read by couples in call / response format. She reads a line, he reads a line, and they read the last line together in unison. This is the plan for my wedding ceremony and I likewise share it with you for the glory of God. May you be blessed by them and through them in like manner for your new life and future together, or as an individual in waiting and appreciative of love / romance. God has taken out great care to design and form these couples, pulling the rib out of his chest and forming specifically the wife that unlocks favor and blessings designed specifically for them. Powers, characteristics, and strengths come from their union that would not otherwise exist or be visible in the world. This only happens when we accept God's choice and submit to God's plan. As God recently said to me, "The truth is intended to set us free. Whether we accept it or reject it, it doesn't change the fact that it's the truth. It is what it is." May your ears be open to what God has to speak for you and you embrace willingly what God has planned for you as a blessing. Let go of being you, and cheerfully submit to "becoming us" in your divinely designed reality.

Devenir Nous

Among the Sea of People

A shard of light piercing a dark room
Leaving the shape of a smile
Sincerely in the wake of its path

Loneliness flees and companionship takes its place
Quickly, willingly breaking that silhouette darkness
tried to produce
Can't look back now

There's no past to remember
Erased in the faint whisper
Of a man who speaks as well as listens

Speak again, my love
Until then…I will wait in the silence
Awaiting those words of forever
To escape the kiss of your lips

Granting freedom to my heart
And the molding of my spirit
With yours in one…

A Dedication

Just as the sun comes up for dawn
And sets again for night
Or like the sun shines every day, but isn't always bright

So shall I be for you

As rain will fall
And soak the earth
Or newborn babies cry at birth

My love is always true

Much better than a summer day
Or happy children
out to play

It isn't based on fun

A constant river
Flowing free
A fountain spring
Eternally

It's from His only Son

A brighter light
Than any lamp
A flame that flickers not
When damp

A love that's based on Christ

Magic Words

I've seen the sun
So beautifully set
Without a trace in the land

So, I'm vowing to cherish
Our every moment
As sure as I stand here a man

The world can become
An ugly place
So, look to me instead

And I will work
At making sure
You'll always lift your head

You have set
Our captives free
When caught in society's clutch

As you shape the clay,

I'm your potter's wheel
Supporting your soft touch

I'm a Kushite King
In a foreign land
And proudly I wear my crown

But I've come to tell you
Of what I need
A Nubian queen in brown

A woman who harbors
A beautiful smile
Reflecting her passionate heart

Who looks at every
Rising sun
As being a brand-new start

She always believes in
Cleaning the slate
And won't give in to strife

And that is why
I need to have
This woman in my life

As I have searched
Both far and wide
I know this to be true

The woman I've been
Searching for
Beloved Queen, is you

Esperance

As I close my eyes and sink into an abyss of loose-
ended emotions and sensation,

The caress of your tender lips coolly brushes across
my skin of chocolate satin,

Warm and welcoming each stain of wetness you
leave on its surface in your kisses.

The waves of electricity stimulate and consume me
in the raging fires of your touch,

Burning me up in the cashmere-like softness of your
fingertips trailing from the crown of

My head along the silky tresses of my hair, trickling
transversely upon my shoulders and

Collecting at the very small of my back···Resting but
a moment

To take a sip of my essence from the bowl of my sacred body in its

Sculpted excellence. With barely enough time to catch a breath, you make me tremble

As you engulf the very cradle of my existence, the mounds of my sensitivity

That serve as the very pillar of my being.

Greedily, you continue to nibble, lavishly drinking the nectar of my sweetness…

My innocence, but not without reciprocation, for even in my blindness

I know where you are.

Reaching out to touch you in just the right places,

Likening unto the very phoenix, to spark life from your fire.

I am the one who floats across the very depths of
your ocean

Like cotton candy melting only to leave a trail of
brown sugar,

The potent sweetness of my love, my life infusing
with yours to make

Lotus-like candy only the privileged may digest.

Such things we do within my heart, without our
hands, but can we only dream to project

Such love in physical form?

L'Homme Noir

This man we proudly call our brother
Never forsaking one nor the other
Supporting his sisters all the while
Never hesitating to create her smile

Though in our natures
We're diverse
Encouraging each other
In better and worse

Forever we'll stand
Approving of one another
In honor of this man
Whom we proudly
Call our brother

Composed of every color
Black man, my father made
Like the sizes of raindrops
Brother varies in his shade

From deep dark chocolate
To a buttery cream
In every color
He creates a new dream

In every endeavor
You find at least one
The promise of his power
In the setting of the sun

His anointed authority
Subtly fills the sky
Reviving the earth
As the clouds begin to cry

He dominates with the strength
Of a new ocean wave
Yet as the sun sets
He knows when to behave

He rules over the earth
Humbly as he can
But I stand beside him

Honoring my black man

OSA

There is a river flowing from the rock of my heart

We know not where the finish is, and barely see the start,

But what we see is water flowing fiercely cool and clear.

When kindness floats to surface, any roughness disappears.

An ever-flowing river without bound or earthly source,

To stop the flowing water takes a nonexistent force.

Such potency, this water saturates more than the rain;

To soothe the deepest hurts and thus relinquishing the pain.

Few know of its power for it comes from up above,

A constant flowing river is the one that bears my
love.

Unusually this river can restore the dimmest flame

Drink from its waters and you'll never be the same.

Taking Precautions

Come and visit me
If you so desire
But don't step across the threshold
Of my sacred temple

Unless you can lock the door behind you

Don't even dream of touching me
If I have to show you how to please me
Drawing you a map for exploration
In a world you should already know

Pen and paper are not included

Bring them with you,
When you come,
Or don't even bother
To knock on my door

I don't have time to teach you how to draw. I can
draw on my own

But if you can paint
Using only your hands
To paint pictures
Of an internal paradise
Without my description, call me

Then we can talk

Kindling

Love me
Wrap your arms around my very soul
Caressing my spirit
Tempting my mind
To plunge
Into the oceans of mystery
I do

Touch me
Slowly…sliding and gliding
Into the valleys and slopes
Of my sculpted temple
Why not?
You know you want to

Feel me
Open your heart and mind
To a sea of exploration
Traveling in a world of understanding
Few will come to know
Will you?

Hear me
Tilt your head
Allowing your ear
To catch the song
My soft lips sing
Once in a lifetime
Make sure you're listening
I don't repeat

Hold me
Entrench the embers of my fire
Caressing and feeding the flames
Insuring the immortality of our sparks
Never extinguish the fire

Agape

You
There is only you.
For nothing else will do
To ever fill the void so real inside my heart

I
I cannot contain
The peace within the rain
Nor any pain you break away with strength that
cannot be described

You truly blow my mind
You'll always be
Conceivably
My love

Don't ever forget that I
Do love you
Nor ever regret that special time as I think of you
I love you, my love

Thanks for your ever-present stance
Insatiable romance
To which no other thing
Can quite compare

I am always by your side
Especially when I try to hide
My love, you draw me near
So, what have I to fear? I'm not alone.

Splendor

To the question of life, the answer is in living,
The music its fruit and the dance in its giving
Since moments are gifts, a token each one,
An impressionism of expression exuded in sun
True light a composite of every color···
Intricate in its design to leave a mark unique.

In the darkness the light shines more perfectly
Encompassing a greater area of surface
Sprouting forth seeds planted underneath
Producing plants of diverse fruits
To feed and nourish the hungry
And strengthen the weak for a new endeavor

Such is the way of beginnings
And in it was first a dark void
That later gave way to brilliant lights
Awakening.

Ecclesia

One who is beautiful
Equally brave

Living for God
And no longer a slave

Far more than a conqueror
As truth sets her free

A blessed example
Of God's grace to see

She's setting the standard
To love one another

A sister in Christ
And a spiritual mother

A living example of love and His grace
To God be the glory for His daughter's embrace

A vessel for Christ to show that His love
Is the greatest, most powerful gift from above

To be nurtured, honored, and handled with care
And to show everyone that there's plenty to share

Kwesi

I took out a moment to think of you...
The way you make me feel, the way you look to me,
in my mind, and I smile

Smile about the soft silky touches that you trace
across me
Transcending physical into spiritual manifestation;
you move me
Shrouded in the light of your eyes,
I twinkle like the stars I see reflected there

Your diamond, valued far above so much else,
You show me in your works
Leaving me to feel safe, protected, honored,
cherished, and you pray for us...opening the heavens
at your appeal for my benefit.

So easily, you soak me up
Coated and covered in the warmth of your blackness,
sweet milk chocolate smells like honeyed musk and
makes me hungry

Not just in my belly or my body, but in my heart

Hungry or thirsty, depending on the moment,
satisfaction can only be found in the taste
The taste of your juicy lips or the sustenance of
positivity that I find in your words

You birth in me such power that reaches far beyond
your touch and lingers, everlasting impressions in the
sands of my life,
I honor you in this moment of my day, to say
Thank you for being you.

Renewal

A mere grain of sand, a piece of rice, the size of one
tiny seed fallen onto rich fertile soil, hardened in the
midst of weathered times, softened yet in the still
instant moment of spring rain...

I saw it happen; take up root and then begin to grow,
impossibility now come forth to pass, when you
remembered...

My name, no longer seed growing in barren country
flourishing gratefully amongst the very weeds
Designing and determined to uproot and then remove
from me my heritage, my promise, and my love that
comes in season to fertilize and prune among the
thorniest of thorns to soften the most delicate of
flowers

I remember, warmer still, evening summers dancing
in the light of stars reflected in the faces of other
flowers hidden from me in the midst of weeded
plains though fragrant

Still, I smell the words they speak for me to nourish
tiny seed in hardened soil softened by that single
drop of rain to grow a delicately petaled thorny rose
encouraged by the wind to smell as sweet.

Privileged

It's true that there are many things about me that are
not on display and I'm not the type of fish that bites
at every passing hook just because it holds some
kind of bait that may or may not prove to be food.

Another way presented; you can say I am quite
selective...but that doesn't change my quality of color
so that I'm now suddenly batting for the other team.

Since you brought it up, let's make it clearly crystal
so you understand that I am not only heterosexual,
but specifically designed for a very special man.

Why should I respond and entertain every single
male that flashes by and hints at any form of interest
whether it's to see how well I cook, what exactly

shakes when I walk, what size bra my "girls" would sit in, what flavor lollipop I like to suck on? There I said it...why should I entertain every inquiry just because it holds a hint of curiosity?

I don't, because I make decisions based on me, and never based on him. I could give a list of reasons, but I'll just share the highlights for now. I am a woman of commitment and I am consistent. I am the same Nicole at the core that I was when you met me whether I was 4, 24, 16, or 5. My heart is still my heart and the love of Christ controls me (2 Corinthians 5:14). That's my number 1.

If you want to know about me then you need to know that I am a woman of standard. That is not just to say that I am about rules, which I also am, but to also understand that I am a confident woman of God and professional by nature...not just because it elevates me above many in my line of work, but it is about my personality. I have ever been a woman comfortably exercised in self-control, but please don't get it twisted. It by no way leaves me prude or introverted.

I am wildfire, so be careful. I will burn you up if you are not accustomed to working in my type of environment. Your melting point must be above 100 degrees Celsius to function or you need not apply. I have entertained men, but you shouldn't need to see them to believe it to be so. Faith is the substance of things hoped for, the evidence of things not seen (Hebrews 11:1). Point is, you don't need to meet and see every man I encounter. The only one you need to know about is the one that earns my commitment and recognizes its value simultaneously.

I haven't met a man who knew the jewel he held within his hands while still he had a chance to hold it. That has nothing to do with the fact that I am of great value; even if he didn't know the meaning of my beautiful, so I will never settle.

Dawning on my fortieth birthday and yet I am still wildfire; ever burning and powerful for only one capable as an individual to entrench me rather than even try to extinguish and waste all that good energy he would need for later (I promise).

I am holding out for the man to whom I would so willingly submit:
The one who moves for pleasing God instead of himself and would so therefore always also please me in the end
So, I can boldly exercise obedience without hesitation or fear, knowing that my trust in God should be equivalent (Ephesians 5:22).

Any other experience was an educational opportunity and over... I am grateful for what they taught me and they can likewise smile in reflection. When he who knows and recognizes me for the privilege and the honor that I bring comes along, I will announce it from the mountain tops.

That said, just because you didn't see it, know that it's not that deep and keep it moving.

Acceptance

I'm letting go of Valentine's Day. Decided it's alright that I have never had a valentine or love experience. I have a god brother who decided that to leave me in a place where I hated it was a criminality. So, he sent me a giant teddy bear, a card for every year I didn't have one, a gift card for my favorite stores, and flowers (two dozen roses; different colors with poems to tell me why I was special). It was a really large box and that was in college... these days, it would probably be a trailer. "The real one will have to do better than me," he said, "I set the standard." Today, you're bearing witness to the fact that I'm not waiting anymore.

I'm not going to lie and say I'm over it. I'm not, but I have to come to terms with the possibility that he's not coming. We're well past he got stuck in traffic, lost and he needed to find directions. Maybe he just found something he decided was more important to do. He made a necessary adjustment and I fell off his list of priorities. It's cool. I can handle it. I'm a big girl survivor. I will, however, take a moment to share my fantasy before I let it go. Maybe someone else's valentine can use it to make some other woman smile a little brighter.

I wanted a semi-quiet evening with a nice dinner. We'd cook it together. I'm thinking lots of treats that we could put in each other's mouths: chocolate, strawberries, pineapple, and mango set up with a chocolate fountain or a little fondue bowl. We could make a mixed green salad with a bit of dried cranberries and some candied almonds and I could make my home-made Fuji apple salad dressing. Our main course would be my famous shrimp scampi and we could do a bit of lobster tail with steak and grilled asparagus with goat cheese and a bit of pesto. We would feed each other all the while looking into each other's eyes and smiling. Moving on to cleaning up the kitchen would be fun, getting each other a bit soapy and wet but being constructive. I like it and we'll have a bit of music going, definitely salsa. In between our conversations we could dance a bit.

Now it's time for dessert and I can change my clothes. He'll heat up the extra chocolate and bring a bit of honey, just in case, with the rest of our fruit while I put on my bustier with garters and grab a blindfold (definitely stilettos, the ones that bear my name) and I'll put my hair up librarian style. He can take it down if he wants to, but first it's my turn.

I'm going to sit him in a comfortable chair, after I let him watch, me undress him, making eye contact the whole time. Then I'll apply the blindfold because he totally trusts me. Whether or not I tie his hands is undecided. If I don't, He may stop me before I'm finished having fun. Read my lips when I tell you that he will come for me. I promise. Then I suppose it will be his turn. What he does to me is completely up to him. Janet said it best when she said, "Don't want to see but feel the things you're going to do to me." Too bad this is just a fantasy, right? I thought I should remind you before you start catching feelings.

Finally, when we're both wrapped completely in each other's warmth I'll have him lay between my thighs while I read to him from my own book of poetry. We'll talk and share our thoughts until we fall asleep and I would smile with satisfaction to have had the Valentine's Day I always wanted. Thank you for letting me share it with you. Now I can let it go.

Sacrificing Isaac

I remember the way, on the day, that we met. It was instantaneously special and the whole world stopped to bear witness the first time you smiled at me. I remember thinking it was for somebody else, but I recall your light got even brighter when our eye contact became official.

Our first conversation was special, not only because it was the first time, but also at the time you were the only man with whom I would exchange words. I didn't speak to any man because I was afraid of them, but I was not afraid of you.

So, when we started out to speak, we quickly lost the need for words. That's when you felt me in your soul, and I heard you in my mind, so we started to speak for each other...touching one another without using our hands. You reached for me and summoned me, connected in my heart. Then you were afraid; enough to sever every tie and erase it, as if you'd never seen the inside of me, and walked away.

Sometimes I still smile when I think of it. The way we were and how we spoke beyond our words was not a fantasy. And even if it never comes again into fruition, I will make it a point to remember what it felt like to bask at the base of the lighthouse and dance in its light even if it washed away in icy nighttime waters and I remained at the ocean's shore with souvenirs in the form of its debris.

I won't forget the face of beautiful even if it's the only chance I get to see it. For the glance was worth, in an instant, more than a million eternities knowing its possibility without bearing witness. I will remember the moment of warmth in the midst of every other cold and smile back at you.

Inquisitively Yours

As long as I've known you, I've never had to say, outside of my head, what I want because you always know.
You always touched me in every place I needed you to and just as long as I ever needed you to linger.

You are the only one capable of making me such a vocal participant
It would be otherworldly to deny that I miss you...regularly. I wish I had access to you now the way it seemed I used to have once upon a time, but we remember because we do reconnect from time to time and pick right up where we left off as if the time had never passed between us except in our wisdom and gained experience.

Did I have access to you the same way you had to me? I want to ask you periodically. I form the words inside of my mouth but they do not escape me. They stay no matter where my thoughts take me. I had a

dream about you that woke me breathless one
morning and I wished it had been my reality.
You tend to go where the others cannot go.

What's more interesting is that I find myself still
wanting you and only you to be there, but I'm not
entirely sure that it's a place where you want to be or
if you happened to wander in, somehow found the
secret panel in my wall that granted you access to
me. I didn't even know it was there until you (you
heard me correctly I said you) showed it to me.
I didn't even know I had a secret room that any man
could get into and I have only ever wanted to extend
it to you, an invitation to take up residence.

Just in case you wonder why I still love you, maybe
it's because you open up to me like morning glories
responding to the sun's kiss in the start of the
morning.
Is that something you do for every woman or just
me?
You are the only man I want to touch and I want
touching me and that is no accident.

We had our first kiss mentally, once upon a time and you took my breath away.
I couldn't forget it if I wanted to, but I don't.
Somewhere in the course of it, you courted me emotionally and spiritually, then we connected.

It made me want to struggle with you and accomplish every dream we could muster independent and together.
If you want to be Barack Obama, I would volunteer to be Michelle and carry you upon my back to get to everywhere we need to go if it were the only way we had to travel there, and I would volunteer for you and only you, because I love you.

I believe in you and trust you with my life, trust you with my heart, and gifted you, my body.
This brings me back to now where I'm scratching my head...
Could all of this in me be accomplished by accident?

Does your heart belong to me or is it a figment of my imagination?

The question I've been avoiding but wanting to ask to
finally hear the answer outside of my head is do you
love me or is all of this a coincidence?
Please, tell me, and I will rest knowing we had that
conversation that we needed to have to clear the air
between us and I can go back to smelling the
flowers.

Island Life

I think about the quiet moments feeling like they should be filled with noises made by two people and find them empty because there's only one

Where is the other? What's keeping him? I often ponder on this question thinking I know some rendition of the answer, but I really don't because I cannot see.

The future is a secret that has not been disclosed to me. I've seen glimpses but only fragments of a much bigger picture that is out of focus. My eyes can't translate the images.

I hold on to the possibility of a possibility that was shown to me. It was filled with laughter and passion while encompassed by love. When, however, is the question. When does it transition from imagination to reality? Do I get to live the happy life that I've seen in my dreams?

Uninhibited

What beauty lies in darkness
On a quiet evening turned morning
When I cannot see the light of the moon
Nor hear the hum of the stars
Skating and dancing across the sky?

How is it that such music will play
Drawing me from concentration,
Thought and meditation in
A silent room···
My secret quiet closet space
In the midst of a soundless land
A place of peace?

Where may I venture off to rest
When every part of my being
Is in a separate location
Of this fantastic world in time,
Waiting in anticipation···

My mind dwells in the thought

Of speaking to you.
Such things to say and sing
In the presence of unadulterated beauty

The heart lies snuggled up
In your embrace, like a cat,
Nestled up to your body
Warm and safe…
Undisturbed and immobile

My spirit shrouds the very
Quintessence of your being;
Your strength, compassion, and patience
Emanating from you

My body awaits your visitation
Sleeping and yet awake
Venturing slowly about the shell of excitement
We call Pittsburgh, wanting you
Progressively with each passing day

How would you define such an event?
Multiple climaxes, one triggering the other.

Inconceivable to the common man and
Indescribable with any other words.

Mystery

Could you be the man
For which my intricate design began?
In the beginning…

Molding me, shaping me
Burning me, like a pot in the fires
Of a kiln designed to create only the utmost in divine perfection

Perfect only in the eyes of God,
And he for whom I was created.

Images of the same mirror's reflection
Once pure light shines upon the glass
One team, one mind, one flesh

Could you be he?
I wonder
For now, it remains a mystery

Life Unfolding

Understanding mysteries; unknown, untold, and unsolved:
These are prepared for the Chosen One, to be understood by none other but him···the discoverer

He is the one for which such beauty, elegance, and delicacy was designed; molded to complete the half-moons of his hips, and to fill the holes of his flaws with the fulness of my own to form a divine perfection in our union.

Each component finally reunited, although one never truly left the other, for both are one in spirit eternal.

Only he will truly know me. Who better than you to identify self? Do you know? Any contact with that one mirror-image reflection invokes the metamorphosis of mere ember to full-fledged fire inextinguishable;
For what worldly water can dispose of that which is not of the world, but simply visiting?

In the mirror, there is only one reflection.
In her graceful stroll, there is only one shadow.
Both, indicative of the other, prove the beauty of oneness.
Each part infused to form the whole perfect being;

Man and woman, the entity of love…who better to have
Authority over all creation,
Whether flying the sky or creeping upon the earth
For nourishment and strength
Only the soil can provide;

To yield the fruits of power and peace
In man's productivity and constructive nature?
From their fruits will come forth new seeds
To plant in rich soil of warmth emanating

Vapors of sensuosity released
Into an unknown atmosphere
In new dimensions…
New to the viewer, on the outside looking in,

But more than familiar to me, the discovered;
Understood only by he who was designed to behold
me.

Dawn

Unto which road
Shall I place my feet to walk
In which direction shall I turn my head to see your light?

Behold it is the sun…
In your eyes, in your smile
In your heart.

Insatiability

Just enough heat
Or a little too much
Who'd have known such fire
Could come with a touch

Such flames to rise
Beyond control
Surpassing the body
And reaching the soul
How ever could it be quenched?

A single finger
Much trembles to make
To cause a body
To suddenly quake
And slowly but surely
Reaching a close
So near satisfaction
Yet off by a nose
Fact or fiction? Who's to know?

If real, what a story,
But destined to end
Electrical surges
A pleasure to send

Not dreamy or magical
Sexy and sweet
Like a honeycomb dripping
Warm and sticky to eat
Tell me what to do.

If fiction, a dream which I choose not to wake
A trip or a cruise
I will willingly take
Through a fantastic ecstasy waiting to start

Using soul, mind, body
And primarily heart
Happily leaving the book wide open
The answer only comes with time

And tension that will blow your mind
Can it ever end in an explosion of release?

Or must it dwell in the abyss of anticipation…

Forever

Rendezvous

I met him there standing

Beneath an ebony moon divine
He was drenched with power
Glowing like an amber dawn
When there's nothing seen in the sky

Oh, but on Earth
He glows
Enchanting the birds to sing
He comes to me in the velvety blackness of night
Holding me close to his chest

I know his touch
Never too rough, but soft enough
To woo me into the shackles of his caress
His hands they greet me
I know them well. They know when and just how long
I need to be held.

Never too long

Nor ever too brief
But simply filling my cup to the rim
Awaiting my approval

And always being cautious
Not to overflow
Resulting in waste
Drying away unknown

Temptation

Don't look at me,
For in every glance, I see a thousand suns
Set across the waters of a distant land
Where I'm not permitted to dance in the light

Please don't touch me
You set aflame each individual nerve in my body,
Burning my muscles and skin to a cinder
Only to be blown away in a breeze
Rather than swept up into the broom of your strong arms

Never, ever kiss me
Life will paint a portrait
Of hand-mixed oils on a homemade canvas;
Immortalizing the brush of your strong yet tender lips

Unless I can keep you···
Carved into your mold of marble
To coat your ebony satin skin with my chocolate silk
I'd rather not be tempted.

Chocolate

Catch me if you can
As I flow to and fro
Taking in my surroundings as I move

What can I say?
I'm solid, sweet, tempting, tantalizingly attractive,
Addictive, almost···I don't stay around
Long enough for anyone to get hooked.

Melt me if you can control the pace of my diffusion
I shall encompass everything with which I come in contact
Leaving behind a trace of sweetness comparable
To only the most potent brown sugar
Only a taste, an inkling of my essence,
Is necessary to inspire a hunger only I can satisfy.

What do you want me to tell you?
I'm impatient···
Solidly so
Waiting for just the right amount of heat

To melt me irreversibly into transformation
And only an oven can perform successfully.

Necessities

Like solving a puzzle and missing a piece,
If there is no food, you cannot have a feast.
If you have no rhythm, you can't play the drums;
And you can't have five fingers if missing a thumb.

If it's missing a wing, a bird can't fly.
Without air for your heart, it stops beating and dies
The branches of life grow together or wilt
And make up the whole like the parts of a quilt

If you take away one, then its purpose will end
For the parts on each other will always depend.
Unless cells reproduce
There can never be birth

And such is the case
When we speak of the earth

No single thing
Can exist by itself

For everyone comes
In somebody else

If air won't mix with water
We cannot have rain

To provide fundamentals
We need the brain

Not one person can live on his own
So, knowing this fact, we will never be "grown."

The old learn from the young
And the young from the old

When the two come together
They stand as pure gold

Regardless of family, your foe or your friend,
We all need each other and forever depend.

Beloved

An amber dawn climbing the horizon
In all its glory, could never speak my heart
For it must descend and yield to the coming of night
Only to return again on another day

You are my sun across the waters of a thousand seas
Never setting and always shining
Calling forth life
To meet you on the shore

Breezes from Heaven

A single drop of water
Fresh, delicate, common, powerful
Carrying promise in the arms of anticipation
Causing new life to emerge from the flames of the past
Burning off into a cinder

'Tis not the end, but the beginning
Opening doors already unlocked,
But refusing to open until now
Predictable and yet complicated
Simultaneously refreshing and unique

Who would have thought such beauty would come without a face?

Sacred Vows

One last look
A smile, a sigh
A final winking of the eye
Brace myself and dive

Slicing, gliding, gracefully
Silently sensuously floating
Surrounded by time

Space, hope, peace, and promise
Along with change embrace honesty
Filling with pools of power
And envelop the world in a glance

Step after step
Whispers rush by
Planting seeds of confusion and nervousness

Thus begins the saga of life
Merging with pages of foreign thought
Breathing, beating

Discovering life again

Calvary

They gave my Lord a swollen head
Much like a basketball
His eyes fell from the sockets
To blind Him of my fall

They whipped and cut upon my Lord
Creating human mesh
And rained upon the weeping earth
Clumps of my Savior's flesh

And just as if the soldiers failed
To cause my Jesus pain
They forced a crown of three-inch thorns
To pierce my Savior's brain

They spat upon my Savior's head
For humor I suppose
As if it wasn't bad enough
His organs were exposed

They sliced my Savior open

To take my Lord apart
And found the sinning of the world
Had burst my Savior's heart

My Lord endured this torture
He never even cried
And when the soldiers finished
My Lord laid down and died

It seems a great injustice
Just how it seemed to end
But death was not the victor,
For Jesus rose again

And after my salvation,
If I may slide or trip,
Then I become the soldier
Who's standing with the whip

I must be good to Jesus
For He has brought me rest
For me, unworthy of the worst,
He always gave the best

A perfect lamb so holy
To cleanse me He was slain
I must make sure, throughout my life
His death is not in vain.

Woo

Do you remember the day we met?
Somehow, I thought I could never forget and here I barely remember.

I know it wasn't, at first glance,
A *take your breath away* romance to which I'd quickly surrender.

Moreso, I've seen it slow to bloom
To see just me, in crowded room, of some store in the midst of December.

In between the passings, an occasional stare

Should we ever make contact, a smile we could
share simply Platonical splendor.

Small meetings of seeming coincidence
Becoming the nature of incidence to muster many
solutions

And suddenly here I am looking for you
Hoping for sharing a moment or two to an ending of
much satisfaction.

And here, without warning, it's now so much more
You see through my heart and you show what's in
store,
So, I find it's my source of attraction.

Just as we've grown closer, we're drifting away
Without explanation and nothing to say, I'm seeking
you over and over again.

Within every silence, a second, an hour
Through many a novel, a moment of power, I'm
searching the eyes of a gentleman.

But somehow, once lost, I'm suddenly finding the slightest of details
so quickly reminding me of the divination that drew me to you.

For you know me, truly see deep into my soul
Beyond all the pieces of me to the whole, sincerely defining me beautiful

And finally waking I see all anew
The person for which I've been searching is you, the perfected mirror, not man

And even in all my confusion I know
Despite my unclear recognition of slow, it was my dream to be your reflection

…That drives me forward.

My Prayer

I only want to see what you want me to see
Let everything else go far from me
I desire to hear what you want me to hear
Others pass in a whisper, so that your voice is clear
May I touch nothing you don't want me to touch
For everything else just doesn't mean that much

Let me only eat what you want me to eat
Regardless of whether it smells sweet
I just ask, in my life, I can do your will
That my soul will be anchored and peace will stand still

My foundation is built
On the most solid rock
And that you'll call me home
When it's time by your clock

My eyes have been opened
My soul is set free
I just pray that they're used

To be pleasing of thee.

Reflection

Dear Lord my prayer
So not to sway
Progressing me to judgement day
Quite early in my mortal life
Before a mother, friend, or wife to be

Prepare me for the foreign land
I enter crawling not to stand
Surrounded by such people strange
From charcoal black to cream they range, that's me

Not crawling still but scooting now to lift
My eyes and light from dark to sift
I see

The earth gets up and slowly move
From staggered walk to flowing groove
Like rivers flowing honeyed sweet
Fresh fruits instead of rotting meat slowly

Change takes place to build a home

On solid rock instead of foam
To call forth stable from the land
And lift up scooters not to stand

For me
Unmoving strong and firm
In curly waves or straightening perm
Of creamy skin to blackened coal
For youth and wisdom part to whole
To be

Individuals apart from groups
Soldiers constituting the mighty troop
Prepared for war and battle still
To build from weak a stronger will
That's me

A woman now, no longer the girl
Who came in sneakers and twirly curl
From lands afar to grow and learn
Like pottery fired in kiln to burn
I see

Such pressure and daily trials
Would mold and form from earthen vials
The vessels made to offer life
For others newly dipped in strife
Slowly

Regaining the wealthy earth
From which all life came forth in birth
To grow progressively short to tall
The helpless baby began to crawl
For me

A girl to soon progress
In regal and blessed womaness
Adult no longer the gullible child
The ivory rose made tame from the wild to be

From the case of a simple bud
Emerging to life from the potent mud
Producing a flower of delicacy
To yield sweetened fragrances constantly that's me

The fruit of a pulsing life

As sister, mother, friend, and wife
Prepared to go and produce more fruit
For the latter harvest and great pursuit
I see

My place in the cycle of truth
For production of wisdom and powerful youth
Once thought a stranger in foreign lands
Now made familiar to suddenly stand slowly
In the midst of a river that flows with zest
Positioning pieces disturbing our rest
Awakening crowns from their ancient shell
Producing magnificent beautiful Belle.

In Me.

Anchored and Satisfied

In the beginning
The world was one
If they couldn't live together
They preferred to be none

From beyond the clouds
A voice was hurled
It said, "Live and be fruitful. Fill up the world."
Against God's word
Which would cause much strife
These two ate
From the forbidden tree of life.

The fruit they ate
Which sweetened the breath
Brought forth from God
A physical death
Because of mercy and love
No other reasons why
God sent His son
For our sins to die.

He gave His unsoiled life
For atonement of our sin
And was crucified on the cross
With nails through His skin
The pain and suffering He experienced
None of us would bear
But He did it so His father's love
We could have to share

And all we have to do is grasp
God's unchanging hand
To begin our lives of salvation
Our walk to the promised land
I know that Jesus Christ
Is the only way for me

He's the one who gave me life
And died at Calvary
Through Him I've come this far
By faith I've been reborn
And He has washed me white as snow
Instead of filthy and worn

I love the Lord more than life itself
And no one can take Him away
For as long as He'll allow me to
In His family I will stay
To do His will I live
Working night and day
And nothing in this tentative world
Will make me falter away

For there's not a friend
Like the lovely Jesus
Only He can cure spiritual diseases
For no worldly man
Sends you to heaven or hell
He has no power
To cast an evil spell
You can only live
As long as God allows

So do His will
He'll show you how
My soul has been anchored

In a spiritual groove
Where I am satisfied
And no man can remove.

A Painful Truth

Lighter than the wind
Floating through the trees
Brighter than the sunbeam
Shining overseas

Delicate as the wings
On a monarch butterfly
Softer than seen
Through the clearest human eye
Rare like the sweet scent of flowers
In a cool summer breeze
Or seeing uncommon birds
Flying throughout the trees
Of all the things we receive from above
There's nothing more special
In the world than love

A Promise

Why do I love thee
Let me count the reasons
You've allowed me to live
Throughout the four seasons

You lift me up
When I'm pushed down
You smile upon me
When others frown

Throughout my life
The bumpy ride
You're always right there
By my side

Although I sin
You love me still
And help me strengthen
My good will

Thy word is a lamp unto my feet

Especially when I'm tired and beat
Thy word is a light unto my path
And helps me know when not to laugh
For all the blessings
He's sent unto me
A faithful servant of God
I shall be

Unspoken

Tonight, I had a time limit to pour out my soul
and share the contents of my being
So, I needed to prioritize, to make sure
I articulated clearly everything I felt
So, he would understand in ten to fifteen minutes:
How much I love him, how much he mattered to me,
to what extent I valued him,
But I could not. He wouldn't let me…
Just flat out interrupted in the middle of the
presentation of my heart.

He decided he didn't want it before he knew the
details of its preparation,
Purposed especially for…
That doesn't matter anymore since he decided
That he simply doesn't need to give an explanation
for why
Twelve years of experience and understanding would
make a difference.

I didn't get to talk about:

The emptiness I'd felt when he was absent
How I missed him so much that I'd realized I wanted
him
To be present
How I noticed how much I liked the sound of his
voice
When he would wake me and ask if I was sleeping
Just to get my view or have me join with him
In prayer where we connected and uplifted,
Two or three who gathered in His name, so He could
join us
And connect us in commitment for a covenant of
time
That he can't even remember

Tell him how I know he walked through fire
Just to have a conversation
When I didn't even speak to those like him
For my own protection, but for him
I made an involuntary exception
That he doesn't even recognize, because he has
amnesia

Fast forward to a time when his every need
Was what I knew as skill and I shared unselfishly
While every time I seemed to fall
He always had the ability to pick me up,
But did he?

It's irrelevant to say that
In a far more intimately spiritual way
He touched me
Over and over without even raising his hand
Except for once
To place the hair behind my ear
And help me with my coat
Just because he knew that
I was angry with him
Wanting to get away as quickly as possible
But this time he insisted on a hug
Before he walked me to my car…

All of it a figment of my great imagination,
Especially since I didn't even like the man
Until we got to know each other better,
Right around the time he started

To speak my mind again.
Or was it my heart?
My every private cry to God
Would find its way back to me
From his mouth.

He told me that he wasn't for me.
God had never purposed him and yet
I'd never spoken anything different;
And even if I'd felt it
In the deepest enclave of my soul,
To gain the favor of God he'd
Have to find her for himself.

And so, I listened while he told me
That it didn't matter how
I knew the content of his soul,
The same way God had showed him mine
The day we met,
And saw the beauty in his flaws
That made him up into the lighthouse that he was
Long before my Father ever told me
That I was the shore

That it was meant to stand on:
Drawing lost and wounded people
Out of dark and chilly waters…
And all the things He had me do
Preparing for Him, because I promised
But ultimately ending in your benefit

And none of that's important
I wasn't even worried about the way you look
Because it's just the giftwrap on the outside of the package
And the contents, so much richer and significant
In value to develop into more sophisticated interest
In romantic nature over time;
Since I had a whole book of ideas to share especially…
But none of that's important anymore
Because you didn't have the time or even patience
To discover for a second what a moment's glance
In simple eye contact could do for you

And now it's gone.
The ship not only sailed, but now it's sunken

And it rests with the Titanic,
Not because I thought it was unsinkable,
But because you decided it was not allowed to float
In less than fifteen minutes.
You created a whole new destiny of silence
That you sealed in your own determination
To reap all that you have sown
So, I diminish…

And release these words unspoken to the winds.

Le Phare (French: The Lighthouse)

He's stood against the storm,
And jagged rocks, but still he stands,
Built up in solid stone
Founded on me.

Against the ragged winds,
the tossing waves,
the darkened sky,
To share unwavered light across the sea.

Inside of thickened darkness
And the coldness of the night,
A warmth from me seeks out through him
Encompassing my light.

A covered path though narrow still,
He shines so others see,
The only way through thistled path
And make your way to Me.

A tenderness in bolder man
He's set aside for Me.
For all the captives broke and bound,
I called him to set free.

Anointing I have spoken forth,
Great hammer set apart
To mold and train My army
He will not break my heart.

Sincerely his heart lights the sea
And guides the wayward ship
To dryer lands and fruitful ways
Ending a restless trip

In wisdom he is well adorned
Behind a youthful smile.
For others who have ventured steps,
I've had him walk the mile.

Though seasons passed and lessons learned
Sought out to do him harm,

I called him out and set apart;
To cold, he's rendered warm.

And as I seek to gain your trust
That you'd receive My love,
For other purpose ordered you,
I've called you from above

Yet you envision others still
To doubt my favored choice.
I am your Father, precious child
Just listen to My voice.

A blessing I have planned for you
With others you will share,
Provided you obey My Words
He'll help to guide you there.

A beacon, He is meant to be
Through which I shine My light,
So those on darkened crooked paths
Would find Me and walk right.

Just one example beyond age,
For him I hold the clock
He stands in waiting up for me,
A vessel on the rock.

Open your eyes in search of light
To draw you out of dark.
Obey and listen to My voice.
Submit and know your mark.

Come heed to My calling here,
To see My wondrous plan for you.
Inside I open secret doors
And share a splendored view.

My child, I promise you are safe
To follow trustfully.
He shines in tribute, bears his heart…
His greatest love is Me.

Majesty

A tender touch···briefly
A glance
Into the depths of a pile of dust

Delicately molded
Into the shape of man
But not nearly a man···

Intricately blackened to perfection
Divinely purposed for power and authority

Black man···
Carrier of music
In his voice

Regulator of rhythm
In the agility of his walk
Standing atop the foundation of family

In his right hand,
Rests respect coupled with compassion

In his left hand,
Love dwells in the midst of maturity

Coating his breast is beauty
Providing protection from the ugliness of the world
In his heart is happiness
For he is a child of the almighty God

He speaks sensitivity
In soft words,
But with conviction

He's crowned with consideration
And his mind is filled
With mysteries only he can reveal
When he wants to do so

He sits on his throne
And never leaves home without his crown

Generosity

Demanding the best of everything at first encounter

Deems itself just if not due to self-worth;

For perfection dwells in places

Far beyond our earthly limitations···mine included.

Truly such things belong to me not because

I'm worthy of any such praise or reward,

But solely on the basis that

My Father wants its privileges for me.

He gives and offers simply 'cause He chooses to do so.

It is my due inheritance because

He claimed me and names me His child.

I become a blessing when I give it back to Him.

May He teach me how to do so properly

Concentration

I knew you.

In a moment's whisper showered in a short exchange of words,

I recognized you for who you are.

Underneath layers of weathered ashes, burned to a crisp shell

On the surface yet living, healthy, soft root buried deep below the cinders.

I know you.

Ivory shimmer of light shows meant to blind you

So as not to see emptiness behind your eyes, you smile.

Trying to cool the natural heat emanating from you.

I feel you.

Cornered in the deepest darkest alley of life all by yourself,

And yet you aren't alone.

Surrounded by the promise of sunshine,

Sharing warmth and vastness to open up the tightness of your chest

And free your heart from bondage.

I know you so well, for we are two sides of the same coin;

Flipping in the hand of circumstance, landing periodically to rest

For but a moment··· before moving on toward that next expense.

In Patience's Virtue

A heavy shroud of darkness ever neatly laying
Must submit and suddenly subside
Upon the presence of the smallest shard of light
Since neither wish to live within the other
So, beginnings come as promised
So they are, and summer's born from
Healthy birthing spring
And winter falls away like shedding skin
To bring about yet another

Within this life, are anew, may joy encompass
Let wisdom thus surround you in your peace
For such accommodations make for autumn beauties
Developing for seasons' passing anticipation
And in due time, comes love with introduction

For happiness and freedom to abide

Si te Voir Seulement

Please don't ask me
To reason why what could
May never be

To perpetuate facades
That rays of sunshine
Aren't warm in their ascension
To the open sky

Those best things in life
Dwell in unanswered questions
Do they not?

Why are we here if not to love?
And yet the curtains draw closer
Before even the beginning
Of a masterpiece materialized

Divinely inspired and created
Even if only for heaven's performance
I will always be thankful for the vision

Embroidered in the satins of my heart

I have finally come to know you

Love, I know your name

As it is written, however could I dare forget?

The Rose

Who would have known a restaurant
Could prove to be such grounds for growth and production?
Soil for the planting of a seed
Doused with the slightest hint of newness
Strangers visiting a new place for the first time

Serving as the fertilizer for our bud to grow
Once planted, we nourish and guard our relationship with care
Nurturing its life for such promise and potential
Watching it grow and suddenly flower…

Opening in the warmth of the sun
Petals shrouded in satin and crème
Light and sweet for delicacy
Deeming them precious and unique
Pink, a mixture of the deepest red
And ivory white
A blend of the utmost sincerity and tenderness
Blessed with immortality

Like our love

Graciousness

For the times I wanted to give
But had naught to offer
And the moments you gave so willingly
While I received so much more

Than you may have purposed to give
Greeted by a thanks short of the depth
Needed to fill the void emanating
In the absence of such a gift…
Forgive me

Commemoration

A special moment on this day
Calls for special words to say
How important you can be
By how much you mean to me
Though busy, buzzing here and there,
I want to let you know I care
Not just right now, but every day
Your presence takes my blues away

So much that I don't want to know
How life would be if you would go
Away from you without your smile
Transforms an inch to be a mile

And silent times to darker days
Without your voice and pleasant ways
So, I've decided on this day
To take time out and now to say

I truly cherish having you
Your company uplifts us two

To heights that reach beyond the mind
Where greatness waits for us to find
Each other

Something to Remember

For she is the dawn,
The new beginnings of my love
Far greater than all the others
Since it comes from me above

Designed in such perfection
As your likeness is in me
An ever-flowing river
For I love abundantly

So, on this day of Valentine's,
And every day beyond,
Remember that my love for you
Will always be the dawn…

To rise up full of warmth and life
And lift you up when tired
A promise from your Father God

No coupon soon expired

Who sent for you companionship
Within the Holy Ghost
Despite all other love that comes
I love My child the most

Yearning

Sorrow, like the moon, comes in many phases
But only one sun stretched forth to light the sky
Likewise in our lives we see many different faces
When the genesis approaches there is only you and I

Glancing in the looking glass, I see my own reflection
The other half of me I couldn't reach
And suddenly the poetry that voiced all my affection
Abandons me for simplicity of my speech

Emancipations Expected

Tell me the truth,
Were you really there
As I laid on the floor?
Did you play in my hair?
Did you brush it and trace
All the curves of my face
As if, in forgetting one, you might
Lose a part of yourself?

Does it please you to visit
Every spot that makes me smile
And presently tickle me in
Places that you've only touched in post experience,
So that each impression
Would linger indefinitely?

Is this real or have the limitations
Of my imagination surpassed
The very boundaries of my so human perception?
Could you really speak my thoughts into
manifestation

As if they were merely dust waiting for you to
breathe
And touch the innermost places of my being,
Sculpted so intimately such to be
Your place of habitation
That you dwell in me as if you've been there from the
beginning

Is that real or did I make you up somehow,
An inkling of insanity as yet to come
Or do you truly hold the key
To every mystery that is me
The labyrinth of which you have already
Overcome over and over again
Because you feel in the thrill of its adventure
You are complete and I am full

Or am I fooled into believing virtuality is real
And I am the fruition of some photographic memory
Projecting simply the pages of some novel
Written romantically and read one time too many?

I need to know the truth.

Will you share it with me?
Would you really touch
So intricately the very mold of my design
In a such a way to provoke explosions of euphoria
and anticipation
Simultaneously
Simply at the mention of your name,
And therefore, create one magnanimous hunger
Insatiable for your very existence as a “Key
Component” of my life

Seriously, I’m asking
Did you speak to me and stimulate
A symphony divine
To play such music to penetrate
My spiritual inner ear···
And no one else would hear it but yours truly,
So that even in those times
When I’m surrounded,
Drowning in the sea of people,
I can hear it playing only for me?

Straight up, I need to know

That when you stop to chill
You do remember yet recall such intimate detail
As in the softness of my skin
The taste of my lips, and the
Depth of my eyes
That you yearn for their familiarity
Exclusive to complete your intimate solace

For when the truth is known to me,
I will be free to reciprocate uninhibited…
Allowing me to embrace my need to practice
principalities
Kama Sutra in the context of chapters
Written with each passing moment
That we share in mutual contact
Then it will be "our story,"
Copywritten by the press of our hearts
Intertwined and not available in stores

Revelations

A moment, just a moment in time, allows for such
clarity to find its way to the surface and as it
becomes visible, I'm expecting to see you, hear you,
and feel you in the silence.

Suddenly, I'm excited, not lonely anymore because I
know I'm not alone.
Just because I couldn't see you doesn't mean that
you weren't there with me reaching out and
connecting with me in our spirit.

True oneness goes so far beyond the flesh
One can almost barely begin to imagine, but if they
did, they would know how true it is to say, "Good
things come to those who wait."
How powerful that statement becomes when you
know the truth and the truth was meant to set us
free indeed.

So, in this moment of my liberation, I decide to wait
for you,

Knowing it is for a very good reason that time reaches beyond measure to meet us and make us one.
Our union wasn't meant to be just for a moment or a lifetime but endless and without limitations. How does one prepare for such a blessing and be ready to receive it at the appointed time?

Jesus said that all things are possible for those who believe, but He grants us the capability because He knows we needed it and couldn't reach that top shelf level of standard without Him.
He raised the bar, on our behalf, because He knew we wouldn't be strong enough to lift it unless He did it for us.

Today, I know, because He did then, I could be corrected and changed, from the one who didn't and couldn't, to the one who does and can.
Because I am, I finally get to be your wife, your woman, your one who earns and owns your desire, and loves you completely beyond you and into your very soul

Why? Because it pleases God and concerns me, so He perfected it. It's that simple and I love you. Forever. Amen.

Sure Footing

I want to say things that you'll remember, even while you're away from me and I'm not whispering in your ear. It would be nice if they could make you smile and maybe make your mouth water in anticipation.

Can you imagine what would make you crave my presence until you were with me? Let me learn that secret so that only I can speak it.
Connection is good. Let us have the kind of connection that brings us to the same destinations while we travel in spirit.

We can unify in prayer to bring down every stronghold, light up every dark place, and release to speak only the truth into each other so that it reaches beyond us every time to set surrounding people free.

I need to learn and know what warms your heart and makes you feel appreciated and admired that you

can walk upright and boldly, knowing you are special
and powerfully significant to me at every given time.

With these tools I can touch with hands so that you
recognize every part of my body, even when your
eyes are closed,
You feel, and see, and hear, or smell to know, beyond
a shadow of a doubt
When it is me as well as when it is not.

Then, and only then, can we have intimate
experiences that prove themselves to be tantric
And you will need all that energy, just like I promised,
and I can't wait to manifest it with you
Over and over again, just because we like the way it
makes us feel together: warm, and safe, and one.

Happy Endings

What do you call the one
The very one that God has fashioned and designed you
To know and love exclusively?

Special, definitely so.
There is only one for me to marry, know and bear children with in love

Unique, he certainly is.
When he smiles at me the sun wakes up from slumber and warmth surrounds me like a plush blanket

Unforgettable, for sure.
Since the day we first made eye contact, I have remembered every detail just like it was yesterday.
Twenty-two years of history in my present-day consciousness.

Undeniable, because

He gains the favor of God along with claiming me as his wife,
And all the capabilities of my love come with choosing me for his bride

We are destined for goodness, hope, and a future of provision without lack
And topped with smiles upon smiles while we serve together
In meeting the needs of God's people for the Glory of God

People often say that love doesn't really happen like we see it on the television screen,
But when we allow God to author, produce, and direct the story, it turns out to be so much better in reality without the risk for cancellations.

In the Midst of Things

Can we just take out a bit of time to soak it all in between us
I have been single for a long time, while looking forward to being your wife, I will honestly need an opportunity to de-program and adjust

I want to learn those things I should know, that you get excited about,
So that I may position myself to celebrate them with you,
Whether that's praise & worship at Saturday night service
Or Black & Gold Sunday for the football game

I want to be able to lift your spirits and warm your smile
On those days where sadness might bring a chill
Hopefully while I'm learning you, it might inspire you to notice
Why I long for you and throw you that special glance / touch every time it starts to rain

Or why all those "little" romantic things would
suddenly be so special
Like fireworks, and mistletoe, and flower petals, and
slow dancing

Let's take some time to learn each other,
Where we are and who we are, regardless of where
we have or haven't been
Can we agree to make everything special and
significant until we collectively agree that it's not or
not as much?
I want to be concerned about the things that concern
us together,
So, we might need to spend a bit of time in isolation
together
Talking, staring, smiling, laughing, crying, and
touching each other in all of those places we can't
necessarily go with our physical hands
I want to know you, see you, until you're
irreplaceable for me

Past Sarah, willing to call in a Hagar, for the
blessings that God will release

Will only ever birth from my womb
And however long that should take would be worth it to me

Past Eve, wanting to believe the words of a serpent
Just because he spoke to her when Adam didn't.
I want to speak multiple languages of love
So, we can still talk when you're not ready or willing to use words:
We can speak through music, scripture, food, in other tongues,
Or some combination of all the above at the same time.
Let's commit to not give in to silent treatment
That would send us and keep us in bad head spaces

May I always aspire to love you past myself,
Like Leah, even when your feelings and affections
Fall in other places. Let my consistency speak to you for me
When my words cannot, so that you feel my love.

In this process, let it bring us both to "make our callings and elections sure" between us.
If our foundation is firm, Beloved, and our focus is God
We will not fail, and everything we create in the midst of us,
Will be pleasing in His sight and overflow into our everyday life.

Questions

What's your favorite color?

The very first thing that you asked me, all the way back in the beginning. What did it tell you, I wonder. Had you already studied the biblical significance of colors? Or maybe it wasn't so deep so early into our story. Could you have been just checking to make sure we could dress alike on occasion?

What's your favorite food?

For years I wondered / figured this might be something that we shared in common: Chinese food buffet restaurants and pounds upon pounds of shrimp in the freezer. Whole cases of water in the refrigerator seems to make so much more sense now than it did then.

May I call you tomorrow?

Could I confess for a moment that this of the three was my favorite. How I long for those days when you would call and share your thoughts with me. At some point, it progressed over time to "*Did I wake you?*" How I wish you would wake me, every morning with the sound of your voice or the kiss of your lips, the softness of your touch···and sometimes in the middle of the night, please do wake me.

These days I think about all of the questions I would have liked to ask you but didn't get the chance. When our present catches up with our future, Beloved, let us play a game of questions so that we can make up for lost time and move forward into a beautiful future. Then maybe it will be my turn to wake you in the morning with a smile.

Perfected in Progress

Do you remember that game perfection? I was thinking about it the other day. Colorful sets of intricately cut pieces that fit into each other and form squares (four sides that make up creation just like the number) all loose and scattered, in the midst of chaos, with a set amount of time to find the right pieces that fit (only one for each) and then all of them have to be set into position before the timer goes off or you have to start all over again.

Have you ever considered the possibility that might be a true and visual depiction of us? Cuts and depressions that fit into each other, complementary strengths and weaknesses that come together and fit in such a way that they reinforce the completed structure where independently they would remain incomplete and vulnerable. This was a conversation we started a long time ago, you and I, but I wasn't allowed to tell you that it was God who told me, when you asked. "I don't know why you think that," is more like what you said, but it was God who showed it to me.

One day I will need to be strong for you, while you are weak, and I will smile upon you in spirit, knowing I had a chance to assure your happiness and I went after it fiercely and willingly with all of my being so that you could be strongly happy even if it meant allowing you to be without me. That's how much I love you and that's how much Jesus loves me. So, I suppose that does make it perfect.

Proclivity

What do I know about you?
I know that you absolutely can't stand it when people are not on time. It totally transfigures your face into this seriously upset person that could condemn the whole world with a single look. I never want to be the cause for that look again, the one that lets you know you just broke fifteen laws, all at the same time, don't do that (especially not on purpose).

I'd so much rather be the one who comes to your rescue and fills in the gap to bring the schedule back together and makes sure that everything flows the way it was supposed to and that smile of yours, that melts me (even when I don't want to do it) comes back to your face.

I know that taking care of your temple is super important to you. You've studied the best and worst things to do, kept the poisons away from your body, and you age quite gracefully and slowly, partially because of it, but mostly because God promised me that He'd keep you for me and He shows you what to do even when you don't realize that He's showing you, so that you can stay healthy and full of energy.

You are a man of stamina, but we won't talk about how or why I know that until after we've said, "I do" and agreed to discuss it, regularly and in full expository details. I know that you are not afraid to "Take it to the streets" and even when it requires you to speak in different languages, you are more than willing to go. I will gladly submit to go with you and labor alongside to rescue as many as we can from the dark and cold waters.

In all these things I know, I also recognize this information, concerning you, is just barely scratching the surface. I need to be willing to go at least twelve feet underwater to find out the innermost elements that bring you together and make you tick.
I'm looking forward to solving such mysteries, one day at a time. As I pull out my Nancy Drew hat or pull my hair back into that "librarian" position, know that I am more than willing to invest the time for discovery

and I will always seek the Holy Spirit to grant me understanding.

I understand that "knowing is half the battle" and I'm fixing my strategies to campaign for the win. I am determined to be "Queen of the mountain" when it comes to your heart, so know that I will not give up and I absolutely love a challenge. Besides, you're totally worth it to me, and I have decided to be yours forever, and without question.

Luminaries Reimagined

I had a dream that you left me a trail of lighthouses, miniatures to lead the path to your heart. I saw them and I knew, immediately, that they would lead me to you.

Across time, across darkness, across cold waters, and I would run to get there and finally find myself smiling at you and with you. Finally, to hold your hand and finally to find a safe place wrapped up inside of your strong arms.

It wakes me sometimes in the middle of the night. I wonder at God's direction to look for your messages of light, but I have yet to find them. Once, twice, so far, and then, instead of the great wave of disappointment there is a glimmer of hope in the window. I saw an image of familiarity, not the lighthouse, but I remember the special lighting from the window and here it was for me to see.

This was like the landmark for the palace, sitting just so in position and even though the building itself had yet to be built, it showed me that it was in fact due to reach reality's shore and I would only need to wait for its arrival in patience and hope, waiting on the mountain once again for God to speak, but now I could do it in worship and in praise.

Sometimes I would need to do it silently so I could soak in it and be saturated. I'm charging up just so that I can be superpowered when we finally make contact and set off our own fireworks that light up the sky so bright that all of the lighthouses go out in unison, not because they're broken, but because they're solar powered and they yield to the greater light that they think is the rising sun, but it's our love. Finally welcomed and permitted, finally free and excited, and finally unified in Christ.

Defining Submission

Thirteen years ago, God and I had a conversation about you in my basement. Six years ago, we reconvened, again in the basement, to pick up where we left off and to allow for more clarity. I was complaining to Him about advantages I felt you had over me and how already cocky (I love you) I thought you were. It bothered me, suddenly, that you had all these experiences I never had and knew so many things I didn't know.

Now here comes my Father, telling me you're the only man I'm ever supposed to marry and all the implications that I felt would come with it. I'd never have the privilege / experience of being in a mutually invested romantic relationship, so I had no idea what it was really like to "have a man" and be someone's "lady / woman." Simulated hours seem to work in some places, but it wasn't helping much in this one.

Besides, I had plenty of women telling me that I didn't behave or think like other "women with men" should think and I was disrespectful toward them because I didn't act like I had insecurities and I didn't acknowledge the absence of perfect trust in their relationships.

So, here we are, God and I discussing you and I'm saying that it isn't fair that I've never dated a man before you. "How will I find out what I like and what I don't, what I need and what I do not?" My Father answers me, "You get to date your husband." I love you, Beloved, so I'm going to tell you the truth and confess that I did not get excited about having my husband as the only man I ever dated.

Then my mind went other places, honestly, like sex. I've never experienced an orgasm during intercourse. What if I'm not doing something right? How will I know how to please my husband if I haven't had any practice? Father, I know what you want me to do and I make it a point to be obedient and please my Father, but it's not fair.

I know I sound like a little kid right now, but humor me for a moment. Lots of people got to do it wrong for a while, experience the wrong way, and then turned around to do it right. What about me? I'm just supposed to skip ahead and do it right? But what if I don't like it, what if he doesn't care about how it makes me feel, what if he's so set on the way it worked in some other time with some other person that he doesn't pay attention to what works with me? I'm supposed to just suffer through it because it's the right thing to do? What if I spend all this time waiting / preparing for someone who chooses to be super selfish instead of being concerned about these things that would concern me?

I feel like that's giving him way too much power over me and he already has the advantage. He's older than me, more experienced than me, might actually be the first man on the face of the earth I've ever me who's smarter than me (…wow! The fact that I'm even admitting that is saying a lot), do we really need to give him that much power over me? He gets to control my pleasure and my pain. He gets to rule and

I'm supposed to obey. What if he doesn't care about me? What if he's not concerned about what I want or how I feel?

Father did not answer me for a while and that did not make me feel better. Then He began to show me how the very things that made me nervous / made me worry, that day, I had requested for them specifically a long time ago. I wanted you to be more experienced than me, so that I could feel like I was safe and in good hands. I knew that you would guide me and save us from being "the blind leading the blind" through our first experiences. I was confident that you could make good recommendations for us and that it would bond us to go through them, step by step, experiencing them together…I imagined that you would have this amazing patience when it came to teaching me and experiencing things with me.

More recently, Father has been teaching me that anything I want for you to give to me, I had to be willing to give it to you first. So, He sent me to serve:

Willing heart, open hands, no makeup, no perfume, nothing flashy, keep it simple, move to meet his every need, because I have equipped you, but always ask first···and in the midst of all these things, I came to love you.

Father would tell me that you needed someone to cook, so I would come ready to cook for you, and I would ask you, but you would say "no." I would look at God and scratch my head, because He told me specifically what you needed, but you "had a thing about people with pets cooking for you." So, then you permitted me to buy pizza, and I bought the biggest, best pizza (you wanted cheese) I could find / buy for you. It was called "the python," and I realized that it was actually me who brought along the serpent. Wow!

So, here we come to me meeting your need and having one particularity of my own. I can't eat pizza without salad. So, once again, Father sends me to you, so I might ask permission to buy ingredients and make the salads fresh at your house without pets.

So, you said yes, and I became the Salad Queen (SQ for short). My Father showed me that there was a lesson that He taught me through our experience. He also showed me that you cared enough to listen, and I could talk to you.

So many other things would happen in between to grow me and to teach you, but God showed me how all of it would be used for His glory and our perfection. He spent a lot of time teaching me how to be your wife and a lot of time showing you how to be my husband. In between He worked out our every concern, all of the kinks and bumps, ahead of time, so that bringing us together would allow for our creation of something smooth and very beautiful.

I'm no longer afraid to yield to your power. I'm no longer concerned that you won't see me enough to care about me. I know that you honestly do and that you will. Most importantly, I know that we can talk things through and that we need to make sure that between us remaining consistent, and we both assured for that when we started in prayer, worship, and thanksgiving. I asked for it, way back in college, and you proposed it thirteen years ago, but we both agreed and entered into covenant. Four o'clock every morning it begins for us.

God said, "Creation starts in darkness and moves forward into the light." Once again, there is creation in the number four moving forward into perfection (the number seven). How do we know that it's perfect? Because God said, "Let there be light," and then it was good. Three hours a day is what we promised, and we both go above and beyond, so why would we fail? We won't because God is our focus and firm foundation, so He will drive, we will succeed, and I will submit.

Willingly, cheerfully, I submit and I yield to your honor and authority. I love you with my entire being and I will so long as I draw breath, just like I promised my Father, and now I'm promising you before witnesses today.

In Case of Emergency

The idea of starting a new adventure is exciting. This truly will be different since it will be for two instead of one. That's drastically different from what I've seen and experienced these 48 years. So, how do we switch? The transition may not be so much of a challenge for you, since you've done it before, maybe you liked it, maybe you didn't, this time you get to do it with me.

I've felt like I've wanted this opportunity most of my life, but honestly having it and wanting it are two different things. Putting it another way, there may come a moment or two in life when I feel like I'd want to retreat to a space that's just for me. Only God knows if that's a good thing or not to have. I'm thinking perhaps it should look like a girl's outing or some long chat on the phone with an old female friend.

Not to gripe or complain about those things that should remain privately between our married ears, but more just old school reminiscing, laughing about "back in the day" times with my Bestie would probably do it. Being alone, not counting this present, has always allowed me to feel like I had some elements of my life that were predictably under my control. Perhaps the married moments of frustration will happen in those moments when everything around me is clearly "not" and there's nothing I can do about it.

In my current days, this would lead me to praise breaks, praying in the spirit, or silent worship. In the event that I don't find solace on my own, in one of these places, might I request in advance for you to pray for me? I have been known to have my own "caveman" tendencies and even now I'm learning that I'm not the best person at asking for help, so maybe you shouldn't try to smoke me out either. Praying for me, however, will most assuredly get my attention. Saying out loud, "I love you and I know that everything will be okay" is nice / good to hear but lifting me up to the Author and Finisher of all things is even better.

At the beginning of our story, I made a mistake. I said something wrong before I knew there was a specific way I should speak and without asking God for the right words to say. The last thing I would ever want to do is get so emotional that I would say something to you, without thinking, and get you so upset that you'd feel like you'd have to run laps on the auto train just so you could be alone in the same room with me.

If we have a moment where we don't see eye to eye, so much that it could turn into a misunderstanding, let us now come to an agreement that we will pray for resolution and not let the sun set down on our anger / dispute. Let us resolve to seek God for peace that surpasses understanding so that we can always close our eyes in each other's arms and know it's because we love pleasing God more than ourselves at the end of everything.

Here's Looking at You

For those times we get so caught up in our right now
that we cause each other to maybe feel some kind of
way, there are some things I want you to know.
I didn't just wait for you and hope for you, but I
prayed very specifically for your selection and
existence.
I didn't do that to cause you strife or torment you. I
did it because that's how special you are to me.
I wanted to be ready for you when you came for me.
I wanted to be a blessing to you and make you smile
when you thought of me knowing that you are
important, significant, and beautiful.
I asked God to make sure that we would fit each
other, so you would have peaks for my valleys and I
could have peaks for yours.
I wanted our weaknesses and strengths to combine
forces and make us unshakeable and unstoppable to
get great things accomplished.
I wanted to know your inner being so well that
looking into your beautiful eyes would be whipped
cream on top of a delicious sundae.

I wanted the feel of your skin to be an outward celebration of my inner understanding and eternal connection with you.
I wanted my love for you to have depth and sustenance that would last and enrich not only itself, but others that would find themselves nearby and bear witness.
I wanted us to reach each other within, on such a level, that saying hello and making eye contact could do things to you and me that we could only begin to copy with our hands…things that could reach beyond the limitations of our physical touch.
I wanted it to make things clear for us, from the beginning, so that in those moments when all I do is lay my head upon your chest you know it's because I thanked God personally for every waking second that I could hear you breathe and listen to the sound of your beating heart.
It's because we counted, God and I, every single moment that I had to long for you, your presence in the midst of the absence. I remember every moment that I had to find another source of gratefulness for all the time we had to spend apart.

The prophet once said when you came for me, all the suffering and pain I had endured I wouldn't be able to remember. I remember telling God that "was a lot to forget." It was, but in these moments, I want you to know that I decided you were worth it. It's important to me, no matter how I might temporarily behave, that you are always in the type of headspace that would enable you to remember.

I love you, Beloved, and I always will···From now and all the way into forever, then all the way back to do it again with you.

Andy

As you are my sun
I can only fly to you
Basking in the warmth of your rays
Burning in the splendor of your heat
Eternally

Likening unto the very phoenix
Emerging from the ashes of an earthen fire
New
Giving birth
Giving life
Breathing love

Grateful

For unto us a child was born,
To grow in love and life
And shine a light upon the world
To show a path that would
For otherwise have gone unseen

Who struggled for you,
So, it would be more beautiful
Each time you find a rising sun
And fallen rain
In the midst of an outspoken storm

We live, but not for ourselves,
Our moments of experience
Are seeds to plant and watch

For nourishing
The times of others come
To get their nourishment
In food for thought

He laughed
To share with you
The waking moments
Of remembered past
Hoping to, in time,
Replace the pain of setting suns
With present melodies of liquid sunshine

Our lives are not for us alone,
But gifts from God
To draw us closer
In recognition of our humanness
And limitation

A lesson learned
Through teachings
In another's eyes,
That love surpasses any wall
A human's hands could build
To block the sun.
It shines more bright

And speaks of purpose recognized

I gratefully accept the wisdom
That you breathed into my heart
For family united
Can provide the greatest shroud of light

Leaving the hidden paths discovered
And the darkest moments into dawn
For what the God of peace and love
Has placed on earth to come,
No consequence may ever
Break or set off course,

But only in delay
May it distract us
From the rising sun
Reflected through your eyes.

Made in the USA
Middletown, DE
26 February 2025

71787964R00095